# The Three Little Pigs

# PaRRagon

Bath · New York · Cologne · Melbourne · Delhi
Hong Kong · Shenzhen · Singapore

# Five steps for enjoyable reading

Traditional stories and fairy tales are a great way to begin reading practice. The stories and characters are familiar and lively. Follow the steps below to help your child become a confident and independent reader:

The three little pigs waved goodbye to their mom. They were going to explore the big, wide world.
"Bye bye," called Mom. "And remember, keep away from the Big Bad Wolf!"

4

**Step 1**
Read the story aloud to your child. Run your finger under the words as you read.

**Step 2**
Look at the pictures and talk about what is happening.

**Step 3**

Read the simple text on the right-hand page together. When reading, some words come up again and again, such as **the**, **to**, **and**. Your child will quickly get to recognize these high-frequency words by sight.

The three little pigs set off.

**Step 4**

When your child is ready, encourage them to read the simple lines on their own.

The three little pigs waved goodbye to their mom. They were going to explore the big, wide world.

"Bye bye," called Mom. "And remember, keep away from the Big Bad Wolf!"

# The three little pigs set off.

Soon, the first little pig met a
man pulling a cart full of straw.

"Please can I buy your straw to
build my house?" asked the first
little pig. The man was happy
to sell his straw. He was tired of
pulling his heavy cart!

The first little pig made a house
of straw.

But that night, the Big Bad Wolf
came to the door.

"Little pig, let me in," he called.

"No way!" said the first little pig.
So the wolf huffed and puffed and
blew the house down.

The first little pig ran away.

The second little pig met
a man chopping trees in
the woods.

"Please can I buy some
sticks to build my house?"
asked the second little pig.
The man was happy to
sell his sticks. He had been
chopping them all day!

The second little pig made his
house in no time.

But can you guess who came to the door? The Big Bad Wolf.

"Little pig, let me in," he called.

"No way!" said the second little pig. So the wolf huffed and puffed and puffed again, and he blew the house down.

The second little pig ran away as fast as he could.

The third little pig found
some bricks.

"I'm going to build my
house with bricks," said the
third little pig to himself.

He carried the bricks to
the top of a little hill. He laid
the bricks. He hammered and
sawed. He put on the roof
and the windows and doors.
His brick house took a long
time to build.

The third little pig had
a good, strong house.

No sooner had the third little
pig finished his house, than he
saw the other two little pigs.
They were running as fast as they
could because the Big Bad Wolf
was chasing them!

"Come and hide in here," he called.

The two little pigs came rushing inside, and the third little pig slammed the door shut.

"Go away, you Big Bad Wolf," they shouted. But the Big Bad Wolf wouldn't go away.

"Let me in," he called.

"You can't come in," said the
three little pigs.

So the Big Bad Wolf huffed
and puffed. Nothing happened.
He huffed and puffed again. Still
nothing happened. The Big Bad
Wolf blew so hard he made himself
dizzy. The three little pigs were safe
inside the brick house.

The brick house was too strong
for the Big Bad Wolf to blow down.

"I'm coming to get you," growled the wolf. He started to climb down the chimney.

The three little pigs were cooking a big pot of hot soup on the fire. The wolf came down and landed, plop, in the soup!

"Yow!" he shouted and ran out of the house as fast as he could!

And the three little pigs never saw
the Big Bad Wolf again.